My Very First Winnie the Pooh

Stories by Kathleen W. Zoehfeld
Illustrated by Robbin Cuddy

A Catalogue record for this book is available from the British Library

This edition published in 2001 by Ladybird Books Ltd.
80 Strand
LONDON
WC2R 0RL

A Penguin Company

2 4 6 8 10 9 7 5 3 1

Printed in Italy

http://www.ladybird.co.uk

Contents

Introduction

The stories in this collection share a common goal: to help and encourage children to face up to some common childhood anxieties. As adults, we try to prepare children for new experiences with reassuring words and straightforward answers. But getting them to see problems through the eyes of Pooh and his friends can help because they share the same anxieties, and can pick up tips on how to deal with them. Pooh, being a Bear of Little Brain, is usually the one who poses the big questions, his friends providing answers from a variety of perspectives.

Pooh's First Day at School helps the young child understand that school can be fun, and is not necessarily the frightening place they think it's going to be. Obviously the first day will be an anxious journey into the unknown but reading about all the fun that Pooh and his friends have is sure to help ease a few fears.

Happy New Year, Pooh! is a story about understanding the passing of time and the seasons. Pooh and his friends are sad when there are no more pages to tear off the calendar and they reflect on the year that has passed. They're thrilled to discover there is a new one waiting to be discovered just around the corner!

Pooh Plays Doctor is the perfect story to read with your child before a check up. It is about allaying fears and explaining simple medical instruments and procedures. Once children see that Pooh is just as anxious as they would be, but is brave enough for an injection, a trip to the doctor will hold far fewer fears.

Pooh's Bad Dream tackles the subject of childhood nightmares. A bad dream can be a terrifying experience for a child until it is understood that he is bigger and stronger than any frightening creature he may meet in a dream. After reading Pooh's story, every child will feel a little more secure when closing his eyes at night.

Don't Talk to Strangers, Pooh! is about Pooh and Piglet learning the Stay-Safe Rules. They learn that if they go out on their own, beyond the Hundred-Acre Wood, they must abide by the rules and not talk to strangers. The Stay Safe Rules are printed at the end of the story and it's a good idea to go through them with your child when you've finished reading.

Pooh's Neighbourhood is a warming story about appreciating and cherishing your neighbours. Pooh decides to take a trip around the whole neighbourhood on his way to delivering a present to Piglet. It's good to encourage children to think about the community of which they are a part and to visit and help their neighbours whenever they can.

10

My Very First Winnie the Pooh ™

Pooh's
First Day at School

"School is starting! School is starting!" cried Tigger. "Come on! Don't be late!"

"School?" asked Winnie the Pooh. "What are you talking about?"

"Christopher Robin has a new back pack and lunch box, and he's getting ready for school. We'd better get ready, too!"

"Oh, Tigger," said Pooh. "School is for children. Not for fluff and stuffing like us."

"What do you mean, not for us?" asked Tigger. "Tiggers LOVE school."

"Piglets don't love school," said Piglet thoughtfully. "At least I don't think we do."

"You're right, Piglet," said Eeyore. "This school business – pencils and whatnot – it's overrated if you ask me."

"It sounds fun!" cried little Roo. "Can I go, too?"

"Come along, Roo," said Pooh. "We'll all go and see Christopher Robin. Maybe he can tell us more about it."

Tigger was first to bound through Christopher Robin's door. "Where's the school?" he asked.

"It's about a mile away," said Christopher Robin.

"A mile?" asked Piglet.

"Not in the Hundred-Acre Wood?" asked Tigger.

"If you have to go that far from home, I'm sure school is not a good thing for Piglets," said Piglet.

"We don't have the brains for it anyway," said Pooh.

"You'd all like school," said Christopher Robin. "I'm sure you would. I'll make a classroom just for us."

"Imagine, our very own school!" said Pooh.

"Can we bounce in school?" asked Roo.

"Of course you can little buddy!" said Tigger. "School's the bounciest place there is!"

"There's no bouncing in school," said Eeyore decisively.

"None?" asked Tigger.

"School is for work. There's no time for fun," said Eeyore.

"Oh," said Tigger, in a very small voice for a Tigger. "Maybe school isn't for Tiggers after all."

Just then, Christopher Robin called out, "Time for school!"

"Oh d-dear," said Piglet.

Christopher Robin set up a table with chairs that were just the right size for Poohs and Piglets.

"Let's sing a song first," said Christopher Robin as they gathered around. ***Good morning to Tigger, good morning to Roo. Welcome, all children, good morning to you.*** Now everyone join in!"

"This is fun. Don't you think?" whispered Pooh.

"Shhh," said Piglet.

"Good morning," they all sang.

"If it is a good morning," said Eeyore, "which I doubt."

21

"Well, the first morning at school can be hard," said Christopher Robin. "But I've met my new teacher, and she's really nice. And I know two people already who will be in my class."

"It is friendly to spend your days with friends," said Piglet.

"And we learn things in school, too," said Christopher Robin.

"That may be alright for you," said Pooh. "But we're nothing but stuffing. Do you really think a little schooling will improve us?"

"Oh, yes!" said Christopher Robin. "You can learn your ABCs. It's fun."

Christopher Robin handed out paper and crayons. "Let's all draw pictures of ourselves."

"What does that have to do with ABCs?" asked Tigger.

"The best letters of the alphabet are the ones in our own names," said Christopher Robin. "When our pictures are finished, we can write our names on them."

P ooh chewed the end of his purple crayon. "P-O-O-H," he printed slowly.

"That's very good!" said Christopher Robin.

"P-T," wrote Piglet carefully, whose name was really quite complicated.

Eeyore, who only knew the letter A, wrote "A" under his picture. "Don't know when I've had so much fun," he said proudly. Roo made some quotation marks. Tigger made a squiggle. Everyone did a fine job.

"Counting is easy, too," said Christopher Robin. "Pooh, let's see how high you can stack these bricks."

"1, 2, 3, 4, 5, 6," Pooh counted.

It was turning into a lovely tower. But when Tiggers see towers, they think, "Towers are for bouncing on," and . . .

CRASH!

Down went the bricks.

"Oh," sighed Pooh.

"Tig-ger!" said Christopher Robin sternly.

"Sorry," said Tigger. "All these ABCs and 1-2-3s are fine, but what about fun? What good is a place if you can't even bounce in it?"

"It's true, you can't bounce when your teacher is talking," said Christopher Robin, "but my school has a playground for bouncing in."

"A real playground?" asked Roo.

"Yes," said Christopher Robin. "A real playground with slides and swings and everything."

"I knew Tiggers loved school!" cried Tigger.

But Pooh, whose tummy was beginning to feel a bit rumbly, was worried about something else.

"I hope you're allowed to eat at school,"

"Oh yes," said Christopher Robin. "That's what my new lunch box is for."

"Mmmm," sighed Pooh wistfully.

And then Christopher Robin, who knew his friend very well, said, "I think it's time for a little snack."

He put a big pot of honey on the table, and everyone helped themselves.

"Can we play again tomorrow?" asked Pooh.

"PLEASE?!" cried all the rest.

"Of course," said Christopher Robin. "We'll play every day – as soon as I'm home from school!"

My Very First Winnie the Pooh

Happy New Year,
Pooh!

"December the thirty-first," said Pooh. "Time to turn the page of my calendar." Pooh lifted the December page. "Hmmm." He said as he scratched behind his ear. "No more pages."

"No more months?!" cried Piglet. "That's t-terrible!"

"Oh, Pooh's calendar is just broken," said Tigger. "Let's go and look at mine. Tiggers' calendars are never broken."

Tigger bounced into his house and flipped up the December page. He gasped. His tail drooped. "No more months! What are we going to do?"

"Let's make up a poem to say good-bye to the months," said Pooh.

"It's too sad," said Piglet. "I can't think of anything to say."

"You can't think a poem," said Pooh. "It just has to come to you." He sat down and looked at his paws.

"Good-bye, January, with snow and frost."

"Oh, d-dear," said Piglet, "our whole year is lost!"

"That's good," said Pooh. "It rhymes very nicely."

Pooh continued. "No more February Valentine sweets. Good-bye, March, with winds and sleets."

"Sleets?" asked Tigger.

"Well, you try," said Pooh.

"Tiggers don't do poetry," said Tigger.

"Tiggers can do Tigger poetry," said Pooh.

So Tigger began, "Ahem . . ."

"I'll miss April's drippy rains, and May-sy's crazy daisy chains.

"Did I rhyme it enough?" asked Tigger.

"Yes," said Pooh, "you rhymed it enough."

"This is fun!" said Tigger.

"**I**'m feeling sadder and sadder," said Piglet. He wiped a tear from his cheek.

"You try," said Pooh. "There's nothing like a poem to make you feel better."

"I'll miss June," sniffed Piglet, "when the Wood was green, and, sniff, all the Julys that might have been."

"Been what?" asked Tigger.

"Well . . . warm and picnicky," said Piglet.

"Mmmm," smiled Tigger.

They sat quietly for a while. Then Pooh brightened.

"I think the rest of the poem has come to me," he said.

Good-bye, August, hot and lazy.

Farewell, September, cool and hazy.

October's colours we'll always remember,
And the pumpkin pies of chill November.

Farewell December, we'll miss your cheer –
Our favourite month of all the year!

"We don't need to say good-bye to December," said Tigger. "We're stuck here."

"Oh yes," said Pooh. "I forgot."

Toot, toot! Ring-a-ling-ling! Bang bang!

Piglet, Pooh and Tigger heard strange sounds coming from Rabbit's house.

"Maybe Rabbit's in trouble!" cried Tigger.
"Let's go!"

Rabbit's house was filled with balloons and colourful streamers.

Toot, toot! Eeyore was trumpeting on a little horn.

Ring a ling ling! Rabbit was ringing a bell.

Bangety bang! Christopher Robin was drumming on a saucepan with a wooden spoon while Kanga, Roo, and Owl looked on cheerfully.

"I wonder why they're so happy," said Pooh.

"They haven't heard the sad news," whispered Piglet.

"Well, it's our bounding duty to tell them," said Tigger. He bounced over to Rabbit's calendar and lifted the December page. "I'm sorry to spoil the festivities," he said, "but we seem to have a bit of a problem."

"There will be no more months in the Hundred-Acre Wood," said Pooh.

Piglet wiped another tear.

56

"Well, I suppose it's to be expected," said Eeyore. "Gaiety, song and dance – it doesn't work for everyone, you know."

"Don't worry, Eeyore," said Christopher Robin, "of course there'll be more months."

"There will?" asked Pooh.

Christopher Robin handed Pooh a saucepan and a wooden spoon to bang. "Come on! Help us ring in the New Year!" he cried.

"New Year?" asked Pooh. "You mean we have a whole new year ahead of us?"

"Yes," said Christopher Robin.

"With a new January and a new February?" asked Pooh.

"And a whole new March, April, May, June, July, August, September, October, November, and December?" cried Tigger.

"Yes," said Christopher Robin. "And look, I've got new calendars for everyone!"

"Wow," said Pooh, "they're beautiful!"

"They're fantabulous!" cried Tigger. "This is so wonderful – we should have a party to celebrate!"

"That's exactly what we *are* doing!" said Rabbit. He gave Tigger a horn. "There now – no more moping around! We've got to welcome in the New Year with lots of noise!"

Piglet smiled quietly. He thought about the picnics and pumpkin pies he'd be sharing with his friends in the New Year. "It's a very friendly thing to say good-bye to the old year and welcome in the new one with your friends," he said.

"Yes," said Pooh, giving Piglet a little hug. "That's just the way it should be."

My Very First Winnie the Pooh™

Pooh Plays Doctor

"Christopher Robin says it's time for my animal checkout," said Winnie the Pooh. "He's bringing his doctor's kit to Owl's house now."

"Doctor's kit!" cried Piglet. "Oh, p-p-poor P-Pooh, you're ill!"

"Ill?" said Pooh. "No – I'm fine. Though I must say I am feeling a bit rumbly in my tumbly."

"That must be it, then!" exclaimed Piglet.

"What's it?" asked Pooh.

"Your tummy – it must be sick," said Piglet.

"Is it?" asked Pooh.

"Isn't it?" asked Piglet.

"Well, yes, it must be. I think," said Pooh.

His tummy grumbled and rumbled.

"Oh dear," said Piglet. "Let's go together. It's so much more friendly with two."

"Come in, Pooh Bear!" exclaimed Tigger, who had set up a desk near Owl's front door. "It'll be your turn to see Owl as soon as Roo comes out."

"Christopher Robin, why do I need an animal checkout, anyway?" asked Pooh.

"Silly old bear," said Christopher Robin. "Not an animal checkout, an annual check up. We need to make sure you are healthy and growing. Also, Owl will give you a special injection which will help to keep you well."

"An injection!" said Pooh. His tummy flopped and flipped.

"An injection!" squeaked Piglet. "Oh dear!"

"It's alright," said Christopher Robin. "It'll only hurt for a few seconds, and the medicine in the injection will keep you from getting mumps and measles and things like that."

"Bumps and weasels," whispered Pooh to Piglet. "How awful."

"Awfully," agreed Piglet.

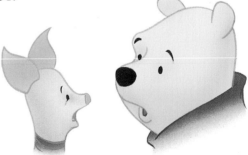

Just then, Roo came bouncing out of Owl's house. "I just had my check up – it was easy!" he said. "I'll have a blue one please, Tigger."

Tigger blew up a nice blue balloon for Roo.

"Come this way, Pooh," said Rabbit, who was being the nurse.

"G-good luck," called Piglet.

Pooh walked hesitantly into Owl's house with Christopher Robin right beside him.

Owl's house felt toasty and warm, which was a very good thing, because Rabbit asked Pooh to take off his shirt.

"Let's sit you up here on the table," said Rabbit.

Rabbit wrapped a wide band around Pooh's arm. He pumped air into the band, and it got tighter and tighter. "How does it feel?" asked Rabbit.

"Tight," said Pooh.

"This gauge tells me your blood pressure is just right," said Rabbit.

"Now, step on the scales, and we'll weigh and measure you . . . Aha! The perfect height for a Pooh Bear of your age, but a bit stout. Still, nothing a little exercise won't cure"

"I do my stoutness exercises every day," said Pooh.

"Excellent," said Rabbit. "Now, if you'll excuse me, I have a great many important things to attend to. Owl will be in to see you in a few minutes."

Owl came in with a flourish. "Well, if it isn't Winnie the Pooh!" he said. "How do you feel?"

"A bit flippy-floppy in my tummy, actually," said Pooh.

"Hmmm," said Owl. "Let's see." He felt Pooh's tummy. He felt around Pooh's neck and under his arms. "Everything seems to be where it should be," he said.

"Oh good," said Pooh.

"Ah, my otoscope is just where it should be, too – just here in my bag," said Owl.

"An oh-to-what?" asked Pooh.

"Nothing more than a little torch," said Owl. "And it will help me see inside your ears . . . mmm . . . your eyes . . . very good . . . your nose . . . excellent . . . and your mouth and throat. Open wide and say ahhh."

"Ahhh," said Pooh. Owl pressed Pooh's tongue down gently with a tongue depressor.

"Lovely!" exclaimed Owl.

80

Next, Owl pulled a small rubber hammer from his bag. "Time to check your reflexes!" he said grandly.

"What's a reflex?" asked Pooh.

"The tiniest tap on the knee, and you'll see," said Owl. Owl tapped Pooh's knee – and his leg jumped.

"Oh, do that again," said Pooh. "That was fun!" And Owl did do it again, this time on the other knee, which made Pooh's other leg jump too.

"Now, this instrument is called a stethoscope," said Owl. "It's made for listening."

"Listening to what?" asked Pooh.

"Your heartbeat," said Owl. "Would you like to hear?" Pooh listened – thump-bump, thump-bump, thump-bump. It reminded him of a poem – a quiet and content poem. And it didn't bother him in the least when Owl said . . .

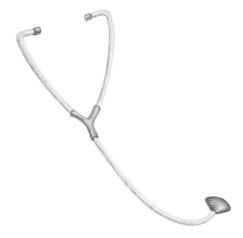

"Sit here on Christopher Robin's lap. It's time for your injection."

"I know it will only hurt for a moment, and it will keep me from getting bumps and weasels," said Pooh bravely.

"That's mumps and measles, Pooh," said Owl.

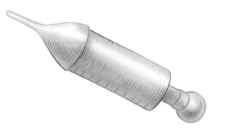

"Could Piglet come in and hold my paw?" asked Pooh.

"Of course he could," said Owl.

W hen Owl had finished, Rabbit popped back in with a plaster. "It'll feel better before you know it," he said, sticking it in place.

"Wow," said Piglet. "You didn't cry once!"

"A check up is no problem for a brave bear like Pooh," said Christopher Robin.

"Pooh, you are a bear in tip-top condition," said Owl, "but that stomach of yours is a little rumbly. I prescribe a large pot of honey the moment you get home. Don't forget to see Tigger on your way out, for a balloon."

"T-T-F-N – ta-ta for now!" called Tigger. "Here's your balloon!"

"Thank you, Tigger," said Pooh. Pooh let Piglet hold the balloon as they wandered off together, towards home and a big pot of honey.

My Very First Winnie the Pooh

Pooh's Bad Dream

W innie the Pooh stood back and admired his work. "Ten new pots of honey," he sighed happily.

"Very nice," said Tigger. "Just make sure that horrible heffalump doesn't come and eat it all up tonight."

"The herrable hoffalump!?" asked Pooh.

"He's a greedy gobbler!" said Tigger.

"You've seen him?" asked Pooh.

"No," said Tigger, "but it's even worse when you don't see him. You can't be too careful when a heffalump's snooping around."

"I'll be careful," said Pooh in a small voice.

"I'll be off then. T-T-F-N – ta-ta for now!"

"Goodnight, Tigger."

Pooh locked his door.

His house seemed rather big and empty.

He climbed into bed and pulled his quilt up over his nose. He stayed like that for a long time.

"Hurrible Hoffalump," he thought. "Must keep watch. . ." He watched and he watched and he watched, until he couldn't keep his eyes open any more . . .

Then, suddenly, his house shook like thunder.
A big red heffalump crashed through the door.
He broke plates, tipped over lamps, stomped to
Pooh's cupboard and guzzled up three pots of
honey.

"Oh!" cried Pooh.

The heffalump turned and looked at Pooh with his horrible green eyes. He snuffled him with his long blue snout. "Ho-ho!" he said. "Now I'm going to eat you!"

The heffalump pushed a honeypot onto Pooh's head.

"Mmppfh!" cried Pooh, with his head inside the honeypot.

He jumped out of bed and reached up to pull the honeypot off his head, but . . . the pot wasn't there! The heffalump wasn't there either.

Where's he hiding? Pooh wondered. He was too frightened to look so he ran to Piglet's house as fast as he could instead.

"Help! Help! A ho-horrible heffalump is ha-hiding in my huh-house," puffed Pooh.

"A huh? A heff? A who?" asked Piglet, rubbing his eyes.

"A heffalump. Hurry!"

Piglet had no time to think. If he had had time to think, he certainly would not be rushing out into the night to help Pooh find a horrible heffalump.

"Come out, heffalump!" cried Pooh.

Piglet grabbed Pooh's broom and held it high over his head.

"Pooh?" asked Piglet, who finally had time to think. "What will we do with the heffalump when we find him?"

Pooh thought and thought and thought.

"Maybe we should go and get Christopher Robin," suggested Piglet.

"Good thinking," said Pooh.

Christopher Robin was in bed when they arrived. "Poor Pooh," he said, "you must have had a bad dream. Heffalumps aren't real."

"He was real," said Pooh. "I felt him snuffle me with his blue snout. He said he was going to eat me!"

"If there is a heffalump in your house, then Piglet and I will help you find him," said Christopher Robin sternly.

"We will? I-I mean, yes, we will," whispered Piglet.

107

Together they went on an expedition to find the horrible heffalump and chase him from Pooh's house forever.

They looked under Pooh's bed.

They looked behind his mirror.

They lifted the tablecloth and peered under the table.

They opened his cupboard. All ten honeypots stood side by side, just as Pooh had left them.

Pooh scratched behind his ear. "It must have been a dream. But why did it seem so real?"

"Dreams can seem real," said Christopher Robin. "But they happen in your mind."

"Oh," said Pooh, "but if I was asleep, how could my mind be making up a heffalump?"

"When you fall asleep your brain stays awake part of the time," said Christopher Robin.

"That's when you're dreaming!" cried Piglet.

"That's right." said Christopher Robin. "Usually dreams are nice, and you forget them when you wake up. But sometimes if you're very tired or worried about something, a dream turns into a bad dream, or nightmare."

"I was a little worried," said Pooh, thinking about what Tigger had said. "And I'm so sleepy. But . . ."

Piglet tucked Pooh into bed.

". . . what if my brain brings the heffalump back?" asked Pooh.

"It's **your** dream," said Christopher Robin.

"You're in charge. If he comes back, just look him in the eye and say: 'Heffalump – go away!'"

"Heffalump go away . . . Heffalump go away . . . Heff . . . go . . . ," Pooh repeated, until at last he was fast asleep again.

Piglet and Christopher Robin tiptoed
out of the house.

Then, suddenly, Pooh's house shook like thunder. A big red heffalump stomped right up to Pooh's bed! "Ho-ho!" he boomed.

"Hoffalump, ga-wah . . . H-Hurrfa lumph hahh!" tried Pooh.

The heffalump was muddled. "What?" he asked.

"Go away," said Pooh quietly.

The heffalump stopped. His bottom lip began to tremble. Tears came to his eyes.

"What's wrong?" asked Pooh.

"I just wanted a little snack, that's all," said the heffalump, "and now, sniff, you're sending me away."

Pooh began to feel sorry he had been so hard on the hungry heffalump. "I'm feeling a bit rumbly in my tumbly, too," he said. "Do you like honey?"

Pooh and the heffalump were soon the best of friends.

Pooh still sometimes dreams about heffalumps, but now they are **always** happy dreams.

Don't Talk to Strangers, Pooh!

One fine day Winnie the Pooh and Piglet were sitting together in their Thoughtful Spot and, when they happened to look up, Christopher Robin was walking down the path.

"Where are you going?" asked Pooh.

"To my grandmother's house for supper," said Christopher Robin.

"You're going out of the Hundred-Acre Wood, b-by yourself?" asked Piglet.

119

"My mum and dad say I'm big enough now," said Christopher Robin. "I know I can do it."

Piglet's ears twitched so hard he had to pull on them to make them stop. "Is-is it safe?"

"Oh, yes," said Christopher Robin, "and it feels great to go out on your own sometimes."

"Not scary?" asked Piglet.

STAY-
SAFE
RULES

"It *was* a little at first," said Christopher Robin. "But my mum wrote down the Stay-Safe Rules for me. Once you know them, being on your own isn't scary at all."

"Can we learn the Stay-Safe Rules?" asked Pooh.

"Maybe *you* can, Pooh," said Piglet, "but it's too hard for a very small animal like me to stay safe."

"You are small," Christopher Robin said, "but you can learn to stay safe, too. The most important thing to remember is – don't ever talk to strangers."

124

"Do you mean people who *look* strange?" asked Pooh.

"Silly old bear," said Christopher Robin, "a stranger is someone you don't know."

"I know Piglet," said Pooh. "And Piglet knows me."

"That's right," said Christopher Robin, "and we all know Tigger, Owl, Rabbit, Gopher, Kanga, and Roo."

"And Eeyore," said Piglet.

"And Eeyore," added Christopher Robin quickly. "They're not strangers."

"Why can't we talk to people we don't know?" asked Piglet. "Are they d-dangerous?"

"Outside the Hundred-Acre Wood there are lots and lots of people," said Christopher Robin.

"Hundreds?" asked Pooh.

"Thousands and thousands," said Christopher Robin. "Most strangers are nice. But a few aren't."

"How can we tell who's not nice?" asked Pooh.

"We can't tell the difference between a good stranger and a bad stranger just by looking," said Christopher Robin, "so we should never talk to any strangers."

"That doesn't sound very friendly," said Pooh.

"You can always be friendly with your friends," said Christopher Robin.

"It's nice to be friendly with friends," smiled Piglet.

"Yes," said Christopher Robin. "But you should never be friendly with strangers."

"Never . . . ," muttered Pooh thoughtfully.

"We can talk more later," said Christopher Robin, hurrying off. "I don't want to be late for supper!"

Well, the word "supper" reminded Pooh that his tummy felt a little bit rumbly, so he invited Piglet over for honey and haycorns at his house.

131

Pooh was just beginning his third pot of honey when Piglet looked up suddenly and listened.

"W-what was that noise?" he asked.

"That's exactly what I was wondering," said Pooh.

"Oh, Pooh," said Piglet, "do you think it's a-a . . . a stranger?"

"It may be," said Pooh. "Sometimes it is, and sometimes it isn't."

*T*ap, tap, tap, went the noise.

"I think it's someone knocking at the door," said Piglet.

"Is that you, Tigger?" called Pooh. But it wasn't.

"Come in, Rabbit!" he said. But Rabbit didn't.

"What if it's just someone with a little pot of honey for us?" asked Pooh as he started to open the door.

"No!" cried Piglet. "What if it's someone we don't know? Remember what Christopher Robin said."

135

P iglet pushed a chair over to
Pooh's window. He stood up
on tiptoe and peeped out.

"It's a very strange
animal," cried Piglet, "with
a shiny yellow head and big
round eyes!"

Pooh looked out, too.

Bang, bang, bang.

The strange animal was hammering nails into a
small board.

137

Pooh started to giggle. "He certainly looks strange, but he's not a stranger. That's Gopher. I forgot that I asked him to come over and fix my sign."

"It'ssss all fixsssed," whistled Gopher as Pooh opened the door.

"Thank you, Gopher," said Pooh. "Won't you come in for a cup of tea?"

"I could cccertainly ussse a sssip," said Gopher, pulling off his hard hat and goggles and wiping his brow.

Pooh had just filled the teapot when there was another knock on the door. "Who's there?" called Pooh.

"It's me, Christopher Robin!" called Christopher Robin.

Pooh opened the door.

"Pooh, you really are a very clever bear," said Christopher Robin.

"Am I?" asked Pooh. "What have I done?"

"You've learned another of the Stay-Safe Rules all by yourself," said Christopher Robin.

"Always make sure you know the person at the door before you open it."

"I had a little help from my friend, Piglet," said Pooh. Piglet smiled proudly.

"Granny gave me a bag of honey cookies to share with my friends," said Christopher Robin.

"You're jussst in time for tea!" said Gopher.

"Mmmm," said Piglet, "your granny makes yummy cookies."

"The best in the world," said Christopher Robin.

"Can we have more tomorrow?" munched Pooh.

"Now that you know the Stay-Safe Rules," said Christopher Robin, "you can come along with me to Granny's house, and we can ask her together!"

CHRISTOPHER ROBIN'S STAY-SAFE RULES

- Don't talk to strangers.

- Never open your door to a stranger.

- Never take a present from a stranger.

- Never get in a car with a stranger.

- If a stranger tries to touch you, shout "NO!," run away, and tell a grown-up you trust as soon as you can.

- And remember, if you're going somewhere, it's always friendlier and *safer* to go with someone you know.

My Very First Winnie the Pooh

Pooh's Neighbourhood

"I say, it's a splendid day in the neighbourhood!" said Owl.

"It's a nice day here, too," said Winnie the Pooh.

"Exactly what I'm saying," said Owl, "a perfectly splendid day in the neighbourhood."

"Which neighbour wood are we talking about?" asked Pooh.

"Neighbourhood," said Owl. "Our neighbourhood – the place where we live and where all our neighbours live and are neighbourly."

"Oh," said Pooh, "it **is** a splendid day in it, isn't it?"

"Quite," said Owl. "Now I'm off for an owl's-eye view!" He flew up and circled around Pooh's house.

"What does it look like from up there?" called Pooh.

"I can see the Hundred-Acre Wood spread out below me," said Owl. "And it's a very lovely sight indeed."

As Owl flew off, Pooh began to think about what it means to live in a neighbourhood, and he thought perhaps he would take a neighbourly present to his closest neighbour, Piglet.

He took a honeypot out of his cupboard and tied a nice blue ribbon around it.

Then he tucked it comfortably under his arm and stumped down the path towards Piglet's house. But when he reached his Thoughtful Spot, which is halfway between his house and Piglet's house, Pooh suddenly had a thought: I could take that path straight to Piglet's house, or – I could go up this path and visit all my neighbours. And sooner or later the path would take me to Piglet's house, anyway.

And so that is what he did.

After he had walked for a time, he came to the house where Kanga and Roo live.

"Hello, Kanga," said Pooh. "I'm just on my way to deliver this neighbourly present to Piglet."

"But, Pooh dear, Piglet lives that way," said Kanga, pointing down the very path by which Pooh had come.

"Yes, I know," said Pooh, "but today I'm going the long way round."

"Oh, I see," said Kanga. "In that case, perhaps you should join us for a snack."

"Come on, Pooh!" cried Roo. "We're going for a picnic!"

Pooh said he was feeling a bit eleven o'clockish; so they all went together up to the picnic spot to share a little something.

Half an hour later, Pooh thanked Kanga, tucked Piglet's honeypot under his arm, and stumped down the path towards Rabbit's house.

"Hello, Rabbit!" said Pooh. "I'm off to Piglet's to give him a neighbourly present."

"If you're going to Piglet's house, what are you doing here?" asked Rabbit.

"I'm going the long way," said Pooh.

"More like the wrong way," said Rabbit. "But since you're here, would you take these carrots to Christopher Robin? I promised he'd have them in time for lunch."

Well, at the mention of "lunch," Pooh noticed that his tummy was feeling the tiniest bit rumbly.

"I'd be happy to," he said.

With carrots under one arm and honeypot under the other, he walked along until he came to the place where the stepping-stones cross the stream.

"One, two, three, four," he counted as he teetered from stone to stone. Eight or nine of Rabbit's friends and relations heard Pooh and peered out of their windows and doors. Pooh shouted, "Hello!" Rabbit's friends and relations waved.

Pooh marched across slopes of heather and up steep banks of sandstone until at last, he arrived at Christopher Robin's door.

"My carrots!" said Christopher Robin happily. "Thanks for delivering them, Pooh."

"It seemed the neighbourly thing to do," said Pooh proudly.

"Would you like to join me for lunch?" asked Christopher Robin.

And Pooh said, "Well, I really am on my way to Piglet's to give him a present. But I don't see why I couldn't stop, just for a little while."

After lunch, and a longish snooze, Pooh was back on his way.

He walked down the path through the Little Pine Wood and climbed over the gate into Eeyore's Gloomy Place, which was where Eeyore lived.

"Hello, Eeyore," said Pooh. "I was just on my way to Piglet's house with this neighbourly present."

"Not coming to visit me," said Eeyore. "I didn't think so. It's been such a busy week already. Why, only four days ago Tigger bounced into me on his way to the river. How many visitors can you expect, really?"

And Pooh, feeling rather badly now, offered Eeyore a nice lick of honey.

He opened the jar, and Eeyore peered in. He looked back up at Pooh.

Pooh peered in. "It's empty," he said.

"That's what it looked like to me," said Eeyore.

"Oh bother," said Pooh.

He stumped off glumly, trying to think how he was going to tell Piglet about the neighbourly present he wasn't going to get after all.

Pooh had almost arrived at the Place Where the Woozle Wasn't and was deciding to take the long path around it, just in case the woozle was, when he saw Owl flying over.

"I've seen the whole neighbourhood today," Pooh told him. "But now I have no neighbourly honey left for Piglet."

"The bees have been busy up at the old bee tree," said Owl. "Perhaps you could fill-up there."

"That's a good idea, Owl, but it's such a long way away," sighed Pooh.

"Come along," said Owl. "We'll take the shortcut through the woods."

So they walked together until they came to a clearing in the middle of the woods, and in the middle of the clearing was the old bee tree. Pooh could hear a loud buzzing near the top.

Up, up, up he climbed.

"Go up higher!" called Owl. "Past the bees. To the very top of the tree. Now, look around you. What can you see?"

The whole neighbourhood was spread
out below him. It was beautiful.
"There's Piglet! He looks hungry." said Pooh.
He filled his honeypot, then he and Owl went
to Piglet's house for supper.

Pooh's House

POOH'S THOTFUL SPOT

Piglet's House

172